Zach & Zoe

and the Bank Robber

Zach & Zoe

and the Bank Robber

by

Kristin Butcher

James Lorimer & Company Ltd., Publishers
Toronto

James Lorimer & Company Ltd. acknowledges the support of the Ontario Arts Council. We acknowledge the support of the Government of Canada through the Book Publishing Industry Development Program (BPIDP) for our publishing activities. We acknowledge the support of the Canada Council for the Arts for our publishing program. We acknowledge the support of the Government of Ontario through the Ontario Media Development Corporation's Ontario Book Initiative.

Cover design: Meghan Collins

The Canada Council | Le Conseil des Arts
for the Arts | du Canada

ONTARIO ARTS COUNCIL
CONSEIL DES ARTS DE L'ONTARIO

Library and Archives Canada Cataloguing in Publication

Butcher, Kristin

    Zach & Zoe and the bank robber / Kristin Butcher.

(Streetlights)

ISBN 978-1-55277-015-3

    I. Title. II. Title: Zach and Zoe and the bank robber. III. Series.

PS8553.U6972Z32 2008   jC813'.54   C2007-907511-8

James Lorimer & Company Ltd.,
Publishers
317 Adelaide Street West
Suite #1002
Toronto, Ontario, M5V 1P9
www.lorimer.ca

Distributed in the
United States by:
Orca Book Publishers
P. O. Box 468
Custer, WA, U.S.A.
98240-0468

Printed and bound in Canada.

For Cole, Brock, and Hunter —
grandsons extraordinaire!

1

On Safari

"Water canteen!" Mr. Dotty called out.

As Zoe and I ran around gathering the items we needed for our trip to the marsh, Mr. Dotty stood in the middle of his garage, checking them off his list.

"Field glasses!"

Zoe hopped over a box of rocks, swerved past a giant stack of newspapers, and slithered between two concrete lions that used to sit at the bottom of a neighbour's driveway. Then she dragged a stool over to the back wall of the garage, climbed onto it, and lifted a pair of dusty binoculars down from a hook.

"Check," she said as she handed them to Mr. Dotty.

"Good," he nodded, slipping them around his neck and ticking them off his list. Then he shouted, "Cameras!" and Zoe and I scurried over to a shelf on the side wall.

"I get the one that folds up like an accordion." Zoe put in her dibs as she tried to elbow me out of the way. We might both be ten years old — we're twins — but I'm still bigger. And stronger. I stepped in front of her and scooped up the accordion camera. Not that I wanted it. It's just that Zoe can be pretty bossy sometimes, and every now and then I need to let her know she doesn't own the world.

"Zach!" she complained. "*I* wanted that one!"

"Too bad," I said, holding the camera out of her reach. "I got it first."

"That's not fair," she pouted and stamped her foot.

I made a big deal of sighing and rolling my eyes. "Sometimes you are such a baby. If you're going to cry, just take it." I shoved the camera into her hands and reached for the shiny black one with the silver flash. Since that was the one I'd wanted all along, it was hard not to smile.

"Check," I said, waving the camera in the air.

"That just leaves our headgear," Mr. Dotty announced as he made his way to the hat pole.

Zoe and I were right behind him. The hat pole is our favourite thing in Mr. Dotty's garage. That and the big wicker basket of masks.

Most people keep cars, lawn mowers, and garbage cans in their garages. Not our back door neighbour, Mr. Dotty. For one thing, he doesn't own a car. Mr. Dotty says cars destroy the ozone, and he doesn't want any part of that. He doesn't own a lawn mower either. But then he doesn't have any grass. From his front gate to his back fence, Mr. Dotty's yard is one big garden — pumpkins, corn, beans, strawberries, and potatoes. The sunflowers are as tall as his house. He doesn't own a garbage can either. What he can't recycle ends up as compost on his garden.

That means Mr. Dotty can put anything he wants in his garage. And he does. It's like a huge treasure chest. Zoe and I visit Mr. Dotty two or three times a week, and we still haven't seen everything in his garage.

As far as garages go, Mr. Dotty's is pretty small. It's also pretty old. The paint is peeling and there's moss on the roof. It doesn't have electricity, so the only light is what comes through a small window. Except when the big wooden doors are open, that is. Then the garage is flooded with light.

It was like that this afternoon. Laser sunbeams were shooting through the shadows, making the sequins on a floppy red hat glitter like diamonds. Zoe went straight for it and plopped it on her head. It was so big, her whole face practically disappeared.

"This is the one I'm wearing," she declared from under the hat's brim.

I circled the pole a few times, trying to decide which hat I was going to choose. There were so many — a top hat, a bright yellow sou'wester, a fire helmet, a fur cap with ear flaps, a sombrero, two cowboy hats, and even a crown! I settled on a soft brown hat like the olden days detectives used to wear. Mr. Dotty said it was called a fedora.

"Which one are you going to pick, Mr. Dotty?" Zoe asked.

"Hmmm," he murmured, walking round and round the pole and squinting up and down. "Let me see." He went around the pole a couple more times. Finally he pulled down a hat, plunked it on his head, and buckled the strap under his chin. It was a safari hat. It even had a mesh veil to keep away the bugs.

"Well, that should about do it," Mr. Dotty beamed. "Backpacks at the ready?"

"Check," Zoe and I chorused as we dragged our packs off an old chest of drawers and lifted them onto our shoulders.

Two white envelopes came with them and fluttered to the floor. Zoe picked them up. "What are these?"

Mr. Dotty glanced at the envelopes and shrugged. "Birthday cards," he said.

"Is it your birthday?" Zoe and I asked at the same time.

Mr. Dotty shook his head. "Not any more, but it was yesterday."

"Happy Birthday, Mr. Dotty," I said. "You should have told us. We would have given you a card too. Maybe even a present."

"So who are the cards from?" Zoe asked. Trust her to be nosy.

"*Zoe!*" I muttered through my teeth. I glared at her too, but she was too busy trying to see through the envelopes to notice.

"That's quite all right," Mr. Dotty chuckled. "One of them is from my boss, and the other is from my sister in Edmonton. Go ahead and look at them if you'd like."

So we did.

The card from the bank where Mr. Dotty works wasn't very personal. The manager's name was just stamped on. But the card from Mr. Dotty's sister made up for it. It was signed seven times! Four times by Madge — I figured that was Mr. Dotty's sister — and three times by Stan. That's Mr. Dotty.

I must have had a puzzled look on my face,

because Mr. Dotty said, "Recycling runs in the family. My sister and I have been sending the same card back and forth for years."

I nodded and looked at the other things inside the card — a lottery ticket and a photograph of the strangest-looking animal I had ever seen.

I turned the picture around and around. "What is it?"

"Let *me* see," Zoe pushed in, making a grab for the photo.

"It's my sister's dog," Mr. Dotty explained. "Madge and I have a difference of opinion about which are better — dogs or cats. So, on my birthday, she sends me a snapshot of Hortense, and on her birthday I send one of Mila."

Just then, Mr. Dotty's cross-eyed Siamese jumped up onto the chest of drawers and meowed. Mr. Dotty scratched her ear. "No need to be jealous, Mila, my princess," he told her. "You are much more beautiful than any dog could ever hope to be." Then with a final scratch under Mila's chin, he cleared his throat and declared, "And now, off to the marsh." He gave his hat a tap and pointed toward the street. "Company forward!"

*   *   *

The marsh is about eight blocks from Mr. Dotty's house. Zoe, Mr. Dotty, and I check it out every few weeks just to see what's happening.

Spring is the best time. Even if you can't see the animals, you can hear them. The whole marsh is a symphony of croaks, chirps, peeps, and buzzes. Summertime is good too, because you can snack on blackberries as you walk around. But summer is also when the mosquitoes are fiercest, and if you've got shorts on, you get eaten alive. The absolute worst time to visit the marsh is right after a rain. That's when the slugs come out, and if you don't watch where you're walking, it's squish city!

"Company halt!" Mr. Dotty commanded when we were still a block away from the marsh.

Zoe frowned. "Why are we stopping here?"

He pointed toward what used to be a big empty field. Now it was a collection of giant holes and mountains of dirt. What little grass was left was being chewed up by an army of bulldozers and dump trucks.

14

Mr. Dotty jammed his hands onto his hips. "What in the world is going on here?"

"*Gggrrrrrmmmm!*" A loud rumbling sound started up behind us. We turned just in time to see a gigantic cement truck backing up.

"Quick, children, out of the way!" Mr. Dotty exclaimed, pulling us backwards along the sidewalk until we bumped into a big sign.

I turned around and read it out loud: "Silver Pond Estates. Luxury Homes at Affordable Prices. Reserve Yours Today."

Mr. Dotty turned back to the bustling construction site. "I'd rather have the field," he said sadly. "This is a big mistake."

I didn't see what was so terrible about it — I love watching bulldozers moving dirt around. But something about the frown on Mr. Dotty's face kept me from saying so. So the three of us just stood there, staring at the field.

Finally Zoe heaved a bored sigh and said, "Can we go to the marsh now?"

"Yes, yes, of course." Mr. Dotty nodded, and suddenly everything was fine again.

At the turnoff to the marsh there's a really steep trail, and Mr. Dotty had to dig in his heels to keep from running down it. Zoe and I didn't even try to walk. We just tore off and waited for Mr. Dotty to catch up.

When he got to the bottom, he was already aiming his binoculars at the trees. "Look," he said. "It's a marsh wren."

Zoe and I squinted in the direction he was pointing. Sure enough, hopping from branch to branch was a puffy little brown-and-black-streaked bird with a white belly.

"Do you think she has a nest up there?" Zoe asked.

Mr. Dotty shook his head. "No. Marsh wrens nest closer to the ground — sometimes right on the grass."

"Like ducks," I suggested. Zoe and I had learned all about ducks in the marsh book Mr. Dotty carries in his backpack. Whenever we want to know something he pulls it out.

"Speaking of ducks," Mr. Dotty pointed down the path, "there's a family of them right now."

Zoe and I hurried toward them. They weren't the least bit scared. They just kept right on quacking and waddling along the wood-chip trail to the pond, as if they were on a crosswalk. One little guy tried to go exploring on his own, but his mother quacked him back into line again. Zoe and I laughed and took his picture.

As we tromped around the marsh, we snapped pictures of everything — well, pretend pictures. We didn't actually have any film in our cameras. We took pictures of the trees and bulrushes, the birds, the bees collecting pollen, and even a little grey rabbit that hopped right in front of us and then disappeared under a honeysuckle bush.

Finally we got to the blue heron part of the marsh. The heron isn't always there, but he was today, and, as usual, he was standing in the water on one leg, as still as a statue. So, of course, we took his picture too.

By the time we left the marsh, Zoe and I must've snapped over a hundred pretend pictures.

2

Pajamas in the Park

Zoe and I do a lot of stuff together. That's partly because we're twins and we've been hanging out since before we were born. It's also because none of our friends live close to us. So when we're not at school, all we have is each other.

On Sunday we spent the afternoon at the park. After tossing a Frisbee around for half an hour we decided to check out the jungle gym. That's when we spotted Mr. Dotty on the other side of the field.

"What's he doing?" Zoe said, tilting her head curiously to one side.

"Beats me." I shrugged. "Slow-motion kung fu, maybe?"

Zoe tilted her head the other way. "But why? And how come he's wearing pajamas?"

I scratched my head. I didn't know the answer to that either. I started across the field.

"Where are you going?" Zoe called after me.

I looked back. "To talk to Mr. Dotty."

"Wait for me!" she hollered and ran to catch up.

At first Mr. Dotty didn't see us. He was concentrating very hard on making these weird poses, so Zoe and I just stood quietly and watched.

"Not only is he in his pajamas," Zoe hissed in my ear, "but he hasn't got any shoes on either. Do you think he's sleepwalking?"

"At two o'clock in the afternoon?" I whispered back.

Finally Mr. Dotty straightened up and turned to Zoe and me like he'd known we were there all along.

"Good afternoon, young G   ᵕ e smiled. "What brings you to   fine day?"

I held up the Frisbee.

"Ah, yes," he nodded. "Frisbee. A fine pastime. Very fine indeed. I haven't had the pleasure in years, but as I recall, it's an excellent means of stimulating one's cardiovascular system."

"Right," Zoe nodded impatiently and then zipped back on topic. "What are *you* doing in the park?"

Mr. Dotty bowed to us. "I was practising the ancient Chinese art of Tai Chi, a kind of yoga and meditation all rolled into one. Very good for the body as well as the spirit. The park is the perfect setting." He spread his arms. "The trees, the grass, the birds, the fresh air and blue sky — it's Mother Nature at her best."

Zoe looked at Mr. Dotty suspiciously. "This tychee thing — you do it in your pajamas?"

Mr. Dotty looked down at himself. "Hmm," he said. "Now that you mention it, my Tai Chi clothes do look a bit like pajamas, don't they?" He shrugged. "Ah, well. The important thing is that they're comfortable."

He dropped down onto the grass, wiggled his

feet into black socks and shoes, and stood up again. Then he took a really deep breath and heaved a satisfied sigh. "I feel like a new person. Now it's time to go home and talk to the plants in my garden. I have to encourage them, you know. They like a good talking to almost as much as compost." He grinned and picked up a couple of bulging cloth bags.

"What's in those?" Zoe asked.

I poked her with my elbow. "Zoe! Mind your own business."

"Mr. Dotty doesn't care — do you, Mr. Dotty?" she argued, turning to him.

"Absolutely not," he agreed. "I have no secrets. Come see for yourself."

He held out the bags and we peeked inside.

"Old bottles, pop cans, and drink boxes?" I said. "Why do you have those?"

He set the bags back on the ground. "They were littering the park. So I just tidied up a bit."

"What are you going to do with them?" Zoe asked.

"Take them to the recycling depot, of course."

Zoe and I rolled our eyes. "Of course."

"I must be off," he beamed. "Enjoy your afternoon, children. Oh," he stuck a finger in the air like he'd just remembered something. "You might want to visit me at the garage later and flex your musical muscles. I have just acquired a bongo drum and a ukulele."

Then, carrying a cloth bag in each hand and out-whistling the birds, he tramped off.

Later that day, we were playing in our backyard when we heard Mr. Dotty open his garage. Remembering how he'd invited us to try out his new musical instruments, we ran off through the gate, across the front lawn, around the corner, and up his driveway. By the time we reached the garage we were puffing.

"Hi, Mr. Dotty," I panted.

"We've come to see your bongo drum and ukulele," Zoe added.

Mr. Dotty was standing in front of a stack of newspapers that came up to his chest. At the sound of our voices, he whirled around. He was white as a ghost.

"I beg your pardon?" His voice was all raspy, like he needed a drink of water, and there were little drops of sweat on his forehead. He was looking in our direction, but it didn't feel as if he was seeing us.

"Are you okay, Mr. Dotty?" I said. "You don't look so good."

He ran his hands through his wispy hair and nodded his head. "Yes, yes, I'm fine. I'm fine. I just didn't hear you coming. That's all." He picked up the newspaper on the top of the pile, folded it, and stuck it under his arm. Then he started to close the garage doors.

"Aren't you going to show us your new instruments?" Zoe asked.

"I'm afraid now isn't a very good time," he said quickly.

"But you told us to come over," Zoe reminded him.

"Did I?" He sounded a million miles away. He started walking toward the house.

Zoe and I exchanged puzzled looks. It wasn't like Mr. Dotty to forget.

"Yes," Zoe called after him. "Today at the park. Don't you remember? You were on your way to the recycle depot and you — "

But Zoe didn't finish her sentence, because Mr. Dotty had walked into the house and closed the door.

3

A Sudden Trip

Zoe and I didn't see Mr. Dotty again until Wednesday morning, when we were on our way to school. He was standing in front of his house, and since he had his bank suit on, I figured he was headed for work. But then I changed my mind. There were two suitcases on the sidewalk beside him.

"Are you going somewhere, Mr. Dotty?" Zoe asked.

Mr. Dotty glanced nervously at the suitcases and then at his watch. Then he smiled at Zoe, but it wasn't his normal smile. This one looked like it hurt. "Ah, yes. Yes, I am." The words flew from his mouth in a big rush. "I'll be away for a couple of days." Then he looked at his watch again and peered down the street.

I thought two suitcases was a lot of luggage for just two days, but I didn't say so.

"Where are you going?" Zoe asked.

Without answering, Mr. Dotty said, "There's my cab. You two had better run along. You don't want to miss your school bus." Then he turned to the yellow cab that had pulled up to the curb.

Zoe and I exchanged surprised looks. Mr. Dotty never took a cab. He either walked or he rode his bike.

The driver jumped out and hurried to open the trunk and load the suitcases.

"Hey, pal. This one's empty," he said as he picked up the second suitcase. "Did you forget to pack?"

Mr. Dotty looked more uncomfortable than ever.

"No ... um ... uh ... no. Actually, I ... uh ... I plan to do some shopping while I'm away," he mumbled, and then dove into the cab.

The driver shrugged and slammed the trunk.

Ten seconds later the cab zoomed away.

*   *   *

I thought about Mr. Dotty all day. Not *all the time*, but lots of times during the day. Like in the middle of social studies when I was colouring a map of Europe and during recess when I was in centre field waiting for somebody to hit the baseball to me.

There was no doubt about it — Mr. Dotty was acting very strangely. For one thing, he was skipping work. Mr. Dotty never skips work. For another thing, he was taking a trip. Mr. Dotty never takes trips. For a third thing, he was going to go shopping! And Mr. Dotty absolutely never, *ever*, goes shopping.

"I think he was lying," Zoe said simply when we talked about it that evening.

"About taking a trip?"

"About everything. Didn't you notice how squirmy he was when we were talking to him? His eyes kept jumping all over the place, and he didn't really answer our questions."

"*Your* questions," I corrected her. I hadn't

asked Mr. Dotty anything.

Zoe rolled her eyes. "Whatever. The point is, he didn't want to talk to us."

"True," I said. "And he's never minded talking to us before."

"Two minutes to dinner, everyone!" Mom called from the kitchen. "Better get washed up."

"I just want to watch the news," Dad called back. "There's been a bank robbery in Winnipeg. The thief got away with almost a quarter of a million dollars."

"You're kidding!" Mom exclaimed, hurrying into the living room with oven mitts on her hands.

"Is a quarter of a mil — ?" Zoe started to ask, but got instantly shushed.

We all listened to the reporter on television.

"The lone robber entered the bank at 4:45 this afternoon, pretending he wanted to use a safety deposit box. He was escorted past security to the deposit box area, located next to the vault. Then, threatening a female employee with what appeared to be a gun concealed in a paper bag, the thief forced her to open the vault.

"After filling a small suitcase with twenty-dollar bills, the thief locked the bank employee in the vault and quietly exited the building. The paper bag was found outside the vault, containing nothing more than a stick.

"Though the thief made a clean getaway, he was caught on film by surveillance cameras."

A fuzzy black-and-white video appeared on the screen.

"That's no help," Dad said. "All it shows is that the guy is skinny, middle-aged, and has thinning hair."

"And he's wearing a suit," Mom said.

"And he's got a suitcase," Zoe added.

The news reporter started talking again. "If you recognize the man seen here, or can give any information leading to his capture, please contact the Winnipeg police."

Mom, Dad, Zoe, and I stared at the television screen as the video continued to play. It felt weird watching a bank robbery in action, even if it had already happened.

The thing is, the thief didn't look like a bank robber. He didn't have a stocking over his head or a mask over his face. He didn't push anybody around and he didn't say anything mean. In fact, he barely talked at all. The only thing he said was, "Would you open the safe, please?" Then, to prove he wasn't kidding around, he pointed the bag-covered stick at the bank lady. When the vault was opened, he handed her the suitcase and motioned for her to go inside and fill it up.

When she was inside the safe, all you could see was the robber's back. That part of the video was pretty boring, because nothing was happening. The robber was just standing there. Finally the lady handed him the suitcase full of money. Then the robber gave her a little thank-you bow and locked the vault with her in it.

As he headed for the exit, he looked up at the surveillance camera.

Mom gasped and then started to laugh. "Oh, my goodness," she said. "If I didn't know better, I would swear that was Mr. Dotty."

Dad chuckled too. "There's definitely a

resemblance, all right. But can you imagine Stan Dotty robbing a bank?"

It was such a goofy idea that Mom and Dad both laughed again.

I didn't though. And neither did Zoe.

4

Suspicious Facts

I don't remember eating supper that night. I can't even tell you what supper was. It could have been pot roast. It could have been macaroni and cheese. It could have been meatloaf. *Heck!* It could have been fried caterpillars for all I know. I don't remember. But whatever it was, I must have eaten it, because when I left the table, my plate was empty.

The thing I do remember about supper is the conversation I had with Zoe. While Mom and Dad were busy talking back and forth in words, Zoe and I were having a silent conversation with our eyes. That's one of the advantages of being twins. We don't always have to say things out loud. Sometimes we just know what the other is thinking. This was one of those times.

And it was pretty obvious Zoe was thinking the same thing I was.

Not even waiting for dessert, we excused ourselves and hurried out to the backyard so we could talk in private.

"That was Mr. Dotty on the news!" Zoe exclaimed, throwing herself onto the wooden seat of the swing. I had to settle for sitting on the edge of a plant pot. "Mr. Dotty robbed that bank!"

"You're jumping to conclusions," I said, though — to tell you the truth — I was thinking the same thing myself.

"You saw that surveillance video," Zoe said. "It was Mr. Dotty! Even Mom and Dad thought so."

"It was somebody who *looked like* Mr. Dotty," I corrected her. "Lots of people look like each other. Besides, the video was fuzzy. And the cameras were way up on the ceiling. We never got a good look at the robber."

Zoe made a clucking sound with her tongue.

"You just don't *want* it to be Mr. Dotty."

"Mr. Dotty is not a thief," I said stubbornly. "Why would he want to rob a bank?"

"Maybe he's poor. Remember how he collected all those cans and bottles in the park and took them to the recycle depot? He got money for them. Maybe he *needed* that money."

"That's crazy!" I hooted.

But Zoe didn't back down. "Think about it," she said. "Mr. Dotty's whole yard is a garden. Maybe that's because he can't afford to buy food at the store. Without a garden, he might starve."

I shook my head. "You're nuts. Mr. Dotty just likes to garden."

"Okay, so how do you explain his car then?"

"Mr. Dotty doesn't have a car," I pointed out.

"Exactly. Every grown-up in Canada has a car, so why not him?"

"Because cars give off harmful fumes and use up the earth's natural resources." I'd heard Mr. Dotty say that at least a hundred times.

"That's what Mr. Dotty *says*," Zoe argued, "but what if that's not the real reason? What if he

34

doesn't have a car because he can't afford one?"

"That's just plain dumb — " I began, but Zoe cut me off.

"And look at his clothes. He wears the same suit to work every day, and everything else he owns comes from the Salvation Army. He never buys anything new. He even recycles birthday cards!"

"So what?" I said.

Zoe rolled her eyes. "Like I said before, maybe Mr. Dotty is poor."

"He has a house and a job," I reminded her.

Zoe shrugged. "Maybe bank tellers don't earn very much money."

"Okay, fine," I said. "Let's say he's poor. Why would he go all the way to Winnipeg to rob a bank? Why not just rob the one he works for here in Victoria? It would be a lot easier."

Obviously Zoe had already thought about that. "So he wouldn't get caught," she said. "If the cameras in Mr. Dotty's bank filmed him, the people he works with would recognize him right away."

She had a point, but I wasn't going to admit it.

Instead I said, "You're forgetting one very important thing."

"What?"

"Mr. Dotty probably wasn't even *in* Winnipeg this afternoon. All we know is that he wasn't here."

"He said he was going on a trip."

"But he never said where."

"It could've been Winnipeg," Zoe insisted.

"*It could have been the North Pole!*" I argued. "Or a jungle in Africa. Or the bottom of the ocean. Mr. Dotty has about as much reason to go to those places as Winnipeg."

Zoe heaved a frustrated sigh. "There aren't banks in those other places."

I rolled my eyes. "Mr. Dotty was probably nowhere near Winnipeg when that bank was robbed. In fact," I had just remembered something, "I bet I know exactly where he went today."

Zoe leaned forward on the swing. "Where?"

"To Edmonton," I announced smugly.

"Edmonton?" Zoe repeated. "Why would he go there?"

"Because his sister lives there. Remember? Mr. Dotty told us that when he showed us his birthday cards. He probably went there to visit her."

Zoe shook her head fiercely. "Uh-uh. If he wanted to visit his sister, he would have done it on a weekend. He wouldn't have missed work to go. Mr. Dotty never misses work."

"He might if his sister was sick."

"Now who's jumping to conclusions?" Zoe grumbled.

"This isn't getting us anywhere," I said. "We need to look at the facts."

"Okay. Fine." Zoe held up a finger. "Fact number one: a bank in Winnipeg was robbed this afternoon."

"Agreed."

Zoe raised another finger. "Fact number two: the surveillance cameras filmed the robbery, and the thief looked just like — "

"The thief looked *a lot like*," I interrupted.

Zoe clucked her tongue. "Okay. The thief looked *a lot like* Mr. Dotty. Fact number three:

Mr. Dotty could have been at that bank." She paused, waiting for my answer.

Reluctantly, I nodded my head. "I guess."

"Fact number four: Mr. Dotty has been acting very strange and secretive lately."

I made a face. "I don't think you can call that a fact."

"Okay, so it doesn't prove Mr. Dotty robbed the bank, but you have to admit he has been acting weird. On Sunday he forgot all about inviting us to his garage to play musical instruments, and he went into his house without even saying goodbye. And this morning, it was obvious he didn't want to talk to us."

I couldn't argue with that.

"Fact number five: the thief carried the money away in a suitcase."

I had no idea what Zoe meant with that one, but I nodded anyway. "Okay."

"Fact number six: Mr. Dotty left here with an empty suitcase. And when the cab driver asked him about it, he got all nervous and said it was for shopping. You *know* that was a lie."

Darn! I'd forgotten about that.

"Well?" Zoe demanded.

"Well what?" I grumbled.

"Is that a fact?"

"Yeah," I agreed. "It's a fact."

"Which leads us to a very interesting question," Zoe continued. "Why was Mr. Dotty taking an empty suitcase with him on his trip?"

"I don't know," I admitted unhappily.

"And another thing — "

I threw up my arms. "What else?"

"Well, remember on the video, the robber was very polite — just like Mr. Dotty. He said, 'Please,' when he made the bank lady open the safe. *And*," Zoe raised her voice when I opened my mouth to interrupt, "he bowed to her when she handed him back the suitcase — just like Mr. Dotty did in the park when he was doing those Chinese exercises in his pajamas."

"Is that it?" I asked.

She shook her head. "Not quite. Did you notice the bank that was robbed was the same company Mr. Dotty works for here in Victoria?"

"What does that prove?"

Zoe shrugged. "I don't know, but there are a lot of banks in Canada. Why pick that one? It seems like a pretty big coincidence if you ask me."

The evidence was definitely piling up against Mr. Dotty. "It doesn't look good, does it?" I frowned.

"Uh-uh. If Mr. Dotty did rob that bank, maybe he won't come back to Victoria," Zoe said.

Just then there was a loud meow, and we looked up to see Mr. Dotty's cat sitting on top of the fence.

"And leave Mila behind?" I shook my head. "There's no way. Mr. Dotty would never do that. He'll be back."

5

Locked!

When the school bus dropped us off Friday afternoon, Zoe and I ran all the way home. Well, not quite all the way home. We slowed down when we got to Mr. Dotty's house.

"Do you see him?" Zoe asked as we peered into his front yard.

I shook my head. "He's not in his garage. The doors are shut."

"Maybe he's in the house," Zoe suggested.

"Maybe," I said. "Or maybe he's not back from his trip yet. He might — "

"Listen!" Zoe cut me off. "Do you hear that? It sounds like a hose. And it's coming from the backyard. Let's go!" Then she tore off up the driveway.

I was right behind her.

Mr. Dotty didn't hear us coming. When we came around the corner of the house and Zoe shouted, "Welcome back, Mr. Dotty!" he jumped right off the ground, and the hose went from watering the peas and beans to watering us.

Zoe squealed. I kind of gasped. Getting blasted with cold water makes you do that.

"I'm terribly sorry," Mr. Dotty apologized, aiming the hose back at his garden. "I was thinking about something and you startled me."

"What?" Zoe said as she shook water off herself.

Mr. Dotty looked confused. "Pardon me?"

"What were you thinking about?"

He frowned. "It doesn't matter."

"How was your trip?" I chimed in, before Zoe could hound Mr. Dotty anymore.

"Fine," he replied, moving deeper into his garden.

"Where did you go?" Trust Zoe to get back to the point.

Don't let it be Winnipeg! I prayed as we waited for him to answer.

"Winnipeg," he said, turning the hose on his potato plants.

I felt my stomach drop into my runners. I looked at Zoe, and she looked at me. Her face said everything I was thinking. This was not good. This was not good at all.

For a few seconds, neither of us knew what to say, but Zoe is never speechless for long. "Were you having a holiday?"

"Not really," Mr. Dotty mumbled.

"Was it a business trip?" I said.

"*Bank* business?" Zoe added, waggling her eyebrows at me.

Mr. Dotty stopped watering his garden and eyed us curiously. It felt like he was reading our minds. I tried to make mine go blank. I didn't want him to know I was thinking he might be a crook.

"Why do you ask?" he said.

Zoe shrugged. "No reason. It's just that most trips people take are either holidays or business.

And since yours wasn't a holiday, we figured it must have been business. And if it *was* business, then it makes sense that it would be bank business, because you work in a bank."

I was impressed. Zoe made our snooping sound very sensible.

I guess Mr. Dotty didn't think so though, because all he said was "Hmmph," and went back to his watering.

But Zoe didn't give up. "So was it?" she called after him.

He looked over his shoulder. "Was what what?"

"Your trip. Was it bank business?"

Mr. Dotty frowned and muttered, "I suppose you could say that." Then he quickly changed the subject. "I hate to be rude, children, but being away for two days has really put me behind. I have a great deal to do. Maybe you should run along home. Your mother is going to be wondering where you are, and you don't want to worry her."

I was stunned. From the way Zoe's mouth

dropped open, she was too. Mr. Dotty had never told us to go home before. *Not ever!*

I couldn't believe it. For a few seconds I stared at him as he went back to watering his garden. Then I nudged Zoe with my elbow. "Come on," I said. "We better go."

She nodded like she was in a trance and turned toward the driveway.

Then *Bam!* She wasn't in a trance anymore. One second she was a walking robot and the next second it was as if she'd been zapped by 2000 volts of electricity.

She ran over to the garage door and pointed. "Look!"

At first I didn't notice anything unusual. The garage looked like it always looked when it was closed. The doors had been pushed shut and an old wooden plank had been placed across them, slung through four rusty metal loops.

And then I saw the padlock. I mean *padlocks!* There were four of them — one bolted at each end of the wooden plank so it couldn't move, and two more clamped around shiny new silver latches at the top and bottom of the doors.

I looked at Zoe and mouthed the words, "It's locked."

She nodded.

"But why?" I whispered. Mr. Dotty never locked his garage. He said it just made thieves think you had something worth stealing.

"Let's ask him," Zoe hissed, and then before I could stop her, she hollered, "Mr. Dotty, why is your garage locked?"

This time the spray from the hose shot straight up in the air, and it was Mr. Dotty who got the shower. He turned off the hose, threw it down on the ground, and stomped over to us.

"I thought I told you to go home!" he barked.

Zoe's eyes got big as saucers. "We *were* going home. But then we saw your garage. It's all locked up, Mr. Dotty. How come?"

"You said you didn't believe in locks," I reminded him.

He grabbed our arms and started walking us toward the street. "It's not terribly complicated, children. I found the locks in my house, so I decided I might as well make use of them."

We'd reached the sidewalk. Mr. Dotty gave us a little push toward our house and then planted himself at the end of his driveway as if he were expecting us to charge back up.

"Say hello to your parents," he said, "and thank your m-m-mother for — "

You could tell he was going to sneeze.

"ACHOO!"

It was a really big one.

"Excuse me," he said. "I think I may have caught a sniffle. Anyway, where was I? Oh, yes. Please thank your mother for feeding Mila while I was away."

Then he reached into his pocket for his handkerchief. Mr. Dotty always carries a handkerchief. He says tissues are an unnecessary waste of the earth's resources. Anyway, as he pulled the handkerchief out of his pocket, something else came with it. Mr. Dotty didn't notice — he was too busy blowing his nose — so I bent down and picked up what he'd dropped.

It was a crisp, new twenty-dollar bill. I rubbed

the smoothness between my fingers, and the twenty-dollar bill suddenly turned into *two* twenty-dollar bills. It was like magic. I held the bills out to Mr. Dotty. "You dropped these."

All the colour drained from his face, and he practically snatched the money out of my hand. "Thank you," he mumbled. Then — without another word — he stuffed the bills back into his pocket and hurried into the house.

6

View from a Tree

A tug-of-war was going on inside me. I liked Mr. Dotty. He was a little weird, but he was nice, and I liked him. In the whole time he'd been our neighbour, he'd never done anything the least bit dishonest. But the evidence was really piling up against him.

If only he hadn't been in Winnipeg when that bank had been robbed! And then there were those crisp, new twenty-dollar bills. And the locks on his garage. It was pretty clear Mr. Dotty didn't want anybody going in there. But why?

"That's where he's hiding the suitcase full of money," Zoe said, as she tried to peek through the cracks of the fence.

"Shhhhh! He'll hear you!"

"He's not even outside," she retorted.

"Yeah, well, he could have a window open or something," I said, and started climbing the tree.

"Where are you going?"

"To the moon," I replied sarcastically.

Zoe isn't easy to discourage. She was right behind me.

I'd climbed that tree so often, I could do it with my eyes shut, and in no time I was higher than the fence. I stopped when I got to a thick branch that stretched over the roof of Mr. Dotty's garage. I straddled the limb and rested my back against the tree trunk. Zoe settled on the branch below.

She poked me in the leg. "What are we doing up here?"

"I don't know about you, but I'm keeping an eye on Mr. Dotty's house," I said, gazing down through the leaves.

"Good idea." Zoe instantly brightened and started peeking through the branches too. "Wow! You can see a lot from up here. It's way better than looking through the fence."

We stared hard at Mr. Dotty's house. I don't know what we thought we were going to see — stacks of money on the kitchen table maybe — but we couldn't even see Mr. Dotty. After a while I got tired of watching and started looking at other stuff, like Mr. Dotty's garden.

From up in the tree it reminded me of the patchwork quilt on my bed. The potatoes made one patch, the corn another, and the tomatoes another. Most of the plants were green, but they were all different greens, so it was pretty cool.

Then I started looking at the moss on Mr. Dotty's garage. It must have been growing there a long time. In some spots it covered the roof completely. It was green in places, yellow and grey in others, brown, and even black, everywhere else. It was so thick and spongy, it looked comfy enough to sleep on. Farther up the roof the moss thinned out, and on the back half of the roof there was just a woolly outline around the edges of the shingles and around —

Around what? I tried to sit up taller so I could

see better, but it didn't help. The roof tilted away from me. I was going to have to get closer. I climbed up to the next branch. It went right out over the garage, so I hung on with my legs and shinnied along it.

"Where are you going?" Zoe called after me. "Do you see something? What do you see?"

"I don't know yet," I called down to her. "I have to get closer."

"Wait for me. I'm coming too."

"No, you're not. The branch isn't strong enough to hold us both. You wait there."

"Well hurry up," she called back impatiently.

I stretched my whole body out and inched along a bit more until I was close enough to touch the roof. What would happen if Mr. Dotty looked out his kitchen window just then? But the tree was so thick with leaves, I didn't think he'd be able to see me.

I glanced down. Right below me was a big shingled rectangle. The edges were thick with moss. I reached out and pulled off a clump. It made a little ripping sound as it came loose. I stared into the crack it left. Then I pulled out another clump, and another. The crack got longer, and when I pulled away the next clump, there was something underneath.

I squinted at it, trying to figure out what it was.

Then, out of nowhere the answer hit me, and boy, was I excited! I wanted to pull out the rest of the moss, but without climbing onto the roof, I couldn't reach it.

I peered through the leaves at Mr. Dotty's house — and nearly fell out of the tree. Mr. Dotty was right there! His back was to the window — so I'm pretty sure he didn't see me — but my heart started pounding like crazy anyway.

I looked back at the hinge I'd uncovered. There had to be another one. I was sure of it. Two hinges attached to a trap door. And a trap door meant another way into the garage.

"Climb down," I told Zoe, as I shimmied back along the branch.

When we were on the ground again, I told her what I had seen.

"Are you sure it's a trap door?" she said.

"Not a hundred percent," I admitted, "but I think so."

Her eyes lit up, and I could almost hear the wheels in her brain starting to turn. "Zoe," I said suspiciously, "what are you thinking?" Her face split into a huge grin. "We can get inside."

"Zoe!" I acted shocked, even though I had been thinking exactly the same thing. "That's trespassing."

She frowned. "No, it isn't. We've been in Mr. Dotty's garage hundreds of times."

"And besides," I said, "even if it is a trap door, it's probably locked."

"Maybe not," Zoe offered optimistically.

I shook my head. "If Mr. Dotty locked the garage doors, why would he leave the trap door open?"

She shrugged. "He might have forgotten about it. It's not like he ever uses it."

"True."

"There's one way to find out," she said, rubbing her hands together.

I felt my eyebrows shoot up. "Are you nuts? Mr. Dotty will see us."

Her grin got bigger. "Not if we do it when it's dark."

7

Tents and Trap Doors

I told Zoe to forget it. Mom and Dad would never let us out of the house at night. Besides, it would be impossible to climb the tree in the dark. I didn't even want to think about standing on that slippery roof. We were just asking to break our necks — or get caught. Maybe both! And for what? The trap door was probably locked. No matter how you thought about it, it was a bad idea.

"Did they catch the fellow who robbed that bank in Winnipeg?" Mom asked as we sat down to supper that night.

Dad shook his head and reached for the bowl of mashed potatoes. "Not yet. The police got a fingerprint off the stick in the paper bag, but there's no match for it in their files. Not that it would prove anything. Lots of people could have touched that stick."

"Wasn't the robber wearing gloves?" I said.

Dad stopped buttering his bread. "You know, Zach, I don't remember." He chuckled. "I guess I wouldn't make a very good detective, would I?"

"I would," Zoe said through a mouthful of carrots. "I notice everything."

Mom laughed. "Be careful you don't break your arm patting yourself on the back."

Zoe frowned. "What does that mean?"

I leaned across the table. "It means you're bragging — again."

She stuck her tongue out at me. Then she turned back to Mom. "Can I sleep out in the yard tonight?"

I nearly choked on the piece of meat I was chewing.

"Whatever for?" Mom said.

"Because I want to. It would be fun."

"Ohhhh," Mom stretched out the word and

made a face. You could tell she was going to say no.

I guess Zoe thought so too, because she instantly started listing reasons why she should be allowed.

"Aw, come on, Mom. I want to try out the tent I got for Christmas. It's the perfect night for it. It's warm, and the weatherman says it's not going to rain. I'll be right in the backyard. It's fenced, so I'll be completely safe. And it's Friday, so I don't have to get up for school tomorrow."

Mom didn't look convinced. "Oh, I don't know, Zoe. I don't like the idea of you being out there all by yourself."

"Please, Mom," Zoe whined. "Please."

Mom was weakening, but she still wasn't quite ready to give in.

"I could sleep out too," I heard myself say.

*   *   *

"I knew you wanted to check out that trap door with me," Zoe gloated later, as we set up the tent.

I sent her my best scowl, "Actually, I'm just

trying to keep you from falling out of the tree and killing yourself." I looked at the roof of Mr. Dotty's garage. "Getting up there isn't going to be easy, you know. Do you even have a plan?"

Zoe stopped hammering the peg into the ground. "What do you mean?"

"Have you thought about how you're going to get up there?"

"The same way you got up there, silly. I'll climb the tree."

"In the dark?"

Zoe frowned. Then her face cleared again and she said, "I'll use a flashlight."

"How are you going to carry a flashlight and climb the tree at the same time?" I snorted.

Zoe glowered at me. "Okay, smarty-pants. What do you suggest?"

So I told her.

* * *

Around eleven o'clock, the back door of the house opened. It was Mom.

"Pretend you're asleep," I whispered to Zoe. Then, because I couldn't stop my eyelids from fluttering, I pulled the sleeping bag over my head.

I heard the tent flap open. Mom was looking inside. What she could see in the dark, I have no clue, but she was looking anyway. Finally the flap closed again and the door squeaked shut as she went back into the house.

"It's about time!" Zoe huffed when the light went out. Then, wriggling out of her sleeping bag, she said, "Let's go."

I grabbed her. "Not yet. We have to wait for Mom and Dad to fall asleep."

Zoe threw herself back down, but every two minutes she popped up again, ready to take off.

"Okay," I said after about twenty minutes. "They should be asleep now. But we have to be quiet. Are you ready?"

She held up the flashlight and nodded.

"Good." I pulled on my backpack. "Follow me."

We slipped out of the tent and crept across the yard to the tree. Then I tied a cord around the flashlight.

"You know what to do, right?"

She nodded.

I took a deep breath. "Okay. Here we go."

I tied the free end of the cord to my wrist, and, with Zoe lighting my way, I started climbing the tree. Partway up, I stopped and tugged on the cord. That was my signal to Zoe to turn off the flashlight and let me pull it up. Then I switched it back on and aimed it at the tree so she could climb. Taking turns, we worked our way up the tree until we reached the branch that stretched out over the roof.

I glanced toward our house. It was dark and quiet. Mr. Dotty's house was dark too.

If I stopped to think about what I was going to do, I knew I'd chicken out, so I just wrapped my legs around the branch and started shimmying along it, while Zoe held the flashlight. When I was over the trap door, I lowered myself down onto the roof.

It was just as slippery as I thought it would be, so I kept a good grip on the branch. Then, crouching down, I started pulling at the moss. It came away without a fight.

"There's another hinge!" I whispered excitedly to Zoe. "It *is* a trap door!"

"Can you open it?" she whispered back.

I cleared away the rest of the moss and dug my fingers under the edge of the door.

It didn't budge.

I tried again. Nothing. I couldn't tell if it was locked or just stuck.

I stood up — still hanging onto the branch — slipped off my backpack, unzipped it, and set it on the roof. Then I sat down and dug around for the chisel I'd borrowed from Dad's toolbox. It was a way better lever than my fingers. When I wedged it into the crack, the trap door moved right away. The sound of wood groaning filled the night. I held my breath and waited for Mom and Dad and Mr. Dotty to come running.

They didn't, so I moved the chisel farther along the groove and pried again. The trap door creaked and complained some more, but I kept working.

And suddenly it came free. It was so unexpected, I almost dropped the chisel.

"I got it!" I squeaked, lifting the door and laying it back against the roof. I stared hard into the opening, but all I could see was blackness.

Zoe sprawled out on the branch and stretched an arm toward me. "Take the flashlight," she whispered.

Cautiously, I reached up and grabbed it. Then I moved back, and waited as she pulled herself along the branch toward me.

I scooped up my backpack, and Zoe held it while I hauled out the rope ladder that had been part of our old swing set. I wrapped the ends around the branch and hooked the metal clips securely in place. Then I dropped the rest of the ladder through the trap door opening. It thumped onto the floor below.

I gulped and looked at Zoe. "Are you sure you want to do this?"

She frowned and nodded. "We have to. It's the only way we're going to find out if Mr. Dotty robbed that bank."

8

A Narrow Escape

I took a deep breath and gripped the rope ladder. "Okay," I whispered. "Here goes nothing."

"Why do *you* get to go first?" Zoe complained.

I squinted at her through the dark. "Because I'm the oldest. You can go first when we cross a minefield."

"Very funny. You better not start looking for the money without me, Zach Gallagher," she grumbled.

"I wouldn't dream of it, sister dearest. Now could you please point the flashlight at the ladder so I can see where I'm going?"

Zoe muttered something I didn't hear, but she did turn the flashlight on.

As I started down into the blackness, I worried that the branch might break or that the ladder would fall apart with me on it. But neither of those things happened. The ladder swayed a little, but it held together just fine, and in less than a minute I was standing on the garage floor.

Then it was Zoe's turn. The instant her feet touched down, she grabbed the flashlight and started shining it around the garage.

"Aim it at the floor!" I growled. "Do you want Mr. Dotty to see the light through the window?"

"Okay, okay. Chill out."

I pointed toward the front of the garage. "Let's start over there. We can work our way to the back."

But we didn't have to. There was a suitcase sitting on the concrete floor right by the big wooden doors. We didn't even have to move anything to get at it.

We stared at each other and then at the suitcase. "Do you think it's locked?" Zoe asked.

I shrugged. "Probably."

While Zoe shone the light on the suitcase, I

knelt down and tried the latches. They didn't move. But looped around the handle of the suitcase was a key. And when I tried it, it worked!

Zoe shook her head. "Mr. Dotty sure doesn't know much about security."

She squatted down beside me and together we opened the latches. Slowly we lifted the lid of the suitcase. I prayed, *please, please, please — let it be empty!*

It wasn't.

Zoe gasped and covered her mouth. I blinked stupidly into the suitcase.

I had never seen so much money in my whole life! The suitcase was full to the brim with wads of cash held together with paper bands and stacked in tidy rows. I wanted to touch them, but I was afraid to.

"Do you think they're real?" Zoe's voice was barely a whisper.

"Well, it's sure not Monopoly money."

"Then it's true. Mr. Dotty did rob that — "

From somewhere back in the garage, a rustling noise cut Zoe off.

"What was that?" She grabbed onto me so hard her nails dug into my arm.

A big lump settled in my throat. I tried to swallow it down. "Is ... is somebody there?" I breathed into the darkness.

At first there was no answer. Just more rustling. And it was getting closer. I swung the flashlight up toward the sound. Two eyes were staring back at me. I was so shocked I fell to the floor, pulling Zoe with me. I looked back to where the eyes had been, but they were gone. I felt something brush my cheek, and I gasped. Then there was a sharp *meow* in my ear.

I turned my head and looked straight into a pair of crossed blue eyes.

"Mila?" I whispered. "Is that you?"

The cat rubbed against my jacket, purring like a motorboat.

I scratched her behind the ear. "What are you doing in here, Mila? You should be in the house sleeping. Does Mr. Dotty know you're out?"

The cat meowed again, louder this time.

"Ssshhhh," Zoe told her. "You don't want Mr.

Dotty to hear you."

But maybe Mila did, because she meowed again.

"We better get out of here," I said, standing up.

"We can't leave Mila," Zoe protested. "What if Mr. Dotty doesn't open his garage for days?"

"He will," I argued. But when Zoe shook her head stubbornly, I gave in. "Okay. Fine. We'll take her with us." I picked up the cat. "You're going to have to ride in here, Mila," I said as I began stuffing her inside my jacket. "I'll let you out when we get on the roof. For now, just sit nice and quiet and enjoy the ride."

But Mila had other plans. With the loudest meow yet, she squirmed loose and jumped. Then there was a humongous crash.

"Oh no," I groaned.

Zoe let out a squeak and rushed over to the little window in the wall. "The light just went on in Mr. Dotty's house!" she wailed. "He must have heard the crash. What if he finds us?" She sounded as scared as I felt.

I swung the flashlight's beam toward the rope.

"Quick," I said. "Climb! When you get to the top, lie flat on the roof and don't move."

"What are you going to do?"

"I'll be right behind you. I just have to lock the suitcase. Go!"

For once Zoe didn't argue. I shone the light at the rope until she was on it, and then I ran back to the suitcase. It felt like my fingers had all turned into thumbs, but eventually I snapped the suitcase shut and locked it. I sprinted over to the rope ladder, stuffed the flashlight into my jacket, and started to climb. Outside I could hear Mr. Dotty undoing the locks.

As I crawled onto the roof, Zoe started hauling up the ladder. Between the two of us, we got it up in just a few seconds. I could tell by the light shining below that Mr. Dotty had the doors open. Quietly, I eased the trap door down, resting it on a piece of the rope ladder so it wouldn't make a noise. It meant the door was still open a crack, but unless Mr. Dotty knew to look, I didn't think he'd notice.

With our noses stuck to the mossy roof and

our ears glued to the trap door, Zoe and I waited. As Mr. Dotty stepped into the garage, Mila let loose another huge meow and came out of hiding.

"Was that you making all that noise, Mila, my princess?" Mr. Dotty soothed the cat. "What did you break?" There was a pause as he looked around. "Ah, that old candy dish. Well, never mind. We'll clean up the mess tomorrow."

Another yowl from Mila.

"Yes, well, I suppose it is my fault for locking you in here. I'll be much more careful in the future. Now let's go to bed."

It got really quiet, and I thought Mr. Dotty must have gone back outside. But then there was a faint *click click*.

Zoe lifted her head. "The suitcase." She mouthed the words.

I nodded. Mr. Dotty was checking out his loot from the holdup. I listened harder. His voice was quieter now, but I could still hear him. And he did not sound happy.

"Oh, Mila," he sighed. "Whatever are we going to do about this money?"

9

The Plan

Even after Mr. Dotty went back into his house, Zoe and I stayed on the roof. It wasn't until the lights went out that we finally climbed down the tree.

"Mr. Dotty really *is* the bank robber!" Zoe moaned as we crawled into our sleeping bags. "I can't believe it."

"What are you talking about? You've been saying all along that Mr. Dotty robbed that bank."

"I know. But I didn't really think he did. I just wanted to solve a mystery. I wanted to be a detective. I wanted to find out where Mr. Dotty went the other day and why he's been acting so funny lately. I thought we were going to find something to prove he *didn't* rob that bank — not that he *did*."

"Yeah? Well, that suitcase full of money in his garage says different."

"But Mr. Dotty can't be a bank robber. He's too nice. He's thoughtful and kind. He likes kids and animals. He cares about the environment. That's not the sort of person who robs a bank!"

I shook my head. It was just like Zoe to completely change her mind.

"You said it yourself," I reminded her. "Maybe he's poor."

Part of me needed to believe that. I needed to believe Mr. Dotty had a good reason for what he'd done. Not that there *is* a good reason for robbing a bank. Stealing is stealing. He'd broken the law, and that meant he was a criminal.

"What are we going to do?" I said.

"What do you mean?"

"I mean what are we going to do about Mr. Dotty? We know he robbed that bank. The money proves it. We have to tell the police."

Zoe gasped. "We can't do that! Mr. Dotty will go to jail!"

I could feel my forehead scrunching up. "I know."

"I don't *want* Mr. Dotty to go to jail!" Zoe wailed.

"Ssshhhh. Do you think I do? But if we don't tell the police, then *we'll* be breaking the law."

"Why can't we just pretend we don't know anything?" Zoe asked.

"Because we *do*."

"I know, but nobody else knows we know."

I shook my head. "It wouldn't work, Zoe. I'd feel too guilty."

"Well *I'll* feel guilty if we turn Mr. Dotty in."

"I don't want him to go to jail either," I said, "but what choice do we have?"

For the next few minutes we just lay in our sleeping bags, staring at the roof of the tent, trying to figure out what to do.

All of a sudden, Zoe sprang up.

"I've got it!" she shouted so loudly I had to shush her again. "I've got it," she repeated more quietly. "We can give the money back."

"Give the money back?"

"Yeah." I could hear the excitement in Zoe's voice. "If we gave the money back to the bank, there wouldn't be a crime anymore. So we wouldn't have to tell the police. It's the perfect plan."

I thought about it. Giving the money back just might work. The police would stop searching for the robber. And though Mr. Dotty would be poor again, he wouldn't have to go to jail.

"I like your idea," I said, "but there's one little problem."

"What?" Zoe demanded.

"The bank Mr. Dotty robbed was in Winnipeg. How are we supposed to get the money back there?"

"We don't have to," Zoe replied. "All we need to do is give the money to the bank Mr. Dotty works for here. They'll get it to the Winnipeg bank."

"We're just going to walk in there and hand over the cash?"

"Yeah. Why not?"

"Think about it," I said. "Two kids walking around with a suitcase full of money. Don't you think people might ask some questions?"

"Like what?"

"Like where did we get it?"

"We could say we found it."

"Where? In Mr. Dotty's garage?" I shook my head. "I don't think so."

"W-e-l-l … " Zoe stretched out the word as her brain got back to work. After a few seconds she blurted, "We could return the money anonymously."

"How? Go into the bank with bags over our heads?"

Zoe glared at me. "Don't be dumb. We could put the money in one of those night-deposit boxes they have outside of the bank."

"You have to have a key for those," I pointed out.

Zoe let out a frustrated sigh. "Well, what do you suggest?"

Shooting down Zoe's ideas was a lot easier than coming up with my own. But if giving the money back to the bank was going to keep Mr. Dotty out of jail, we had to do it. But we had to do it without anybody knowing, so the police wouldn't ask questions and so Mr. Dotty wouldn't find out what we'd done.

But how?

Then it came to me.

"We can mail it to the police," I said. "We'll put the money in a box with a note explaining it's from the bank robbery, and then we'll stick it in a mailbox. The post office will deliver the package to the police, and the police will give the money back to the bank."

It was such a perfect solution I couldn't stop myself from grinning.

"Problem solved," I said happily.

10

Trouble at the Marsh

The next morning I was woken up by somebody shaking my leg. I lifted my head and squinted against the sunlight streaming through the open tent flap.

"Come on, sleepyheads," Mom laughed. "It's almost ten o'clock. Do you plan on sleeping the whole day away? I've made blueberry waffles, but if you don't get to the table soon, there won't be any left. Your father is shovelling them down like there's no tomorrow."

As she disappeared back into the house, I shut my eyes again. The sun was warm, my sleeping bag was warm, and all I wanted to do was drift back to sleep and finish the dream I'd been having. Then I remembered the suitcase full of money in Mr. Dotty's garage, and I was instantly wide awake.

I shook the lump in the sleeping bag next to me. "Come on, Zoe. We gotta get up."

"Go away. I'm sleeping," she mumbled, and rolled over.

"Fine," I said as I pushed my feet into my runners. "I'll just solve the case of the stolen bank money all by myself."

That got her. She sprang straight up and blinked. Her eyes were open, but I could tell she really wasn't awake.

"Nice hair," I snickered. Half of it was hanging in her face and the rest was standing straight up.

"Oh, be quiet," she muttered as she tried to untangle herself from her sleeping bag. After a few seconds, she gave up and flopped back down.

But not even sleep could keep Zoe out of action for long, and by the time I'd washed up and sat down at the table, she'd made it to the kitchen. She still didn't look very awake, but at least she was on her feet.

"Hop into the shower," Mom told her. "That will wake you up. Then you can eat. I'll make sure Dad and Zach save you some waffles."

Mom must have been right about the shower, because when Zoe finally got to the table, she looked almost human.

"How was the camp-out?" Mom asked.

"Good," I said.

"Yeah," Zoe said. "It was fun. Can we do it again tonight?"

Mom passed the platter of waffles. "Again?"

"Yeah." Zoe said. "The tent is already set up, so we might as well use it. Besides, we sleep better in the fresh air. Don't we, Zach?"

"Absolutely," I nodded.

"Well, if that's the case, maybe I should join you," Mom laughed. "I had a terrible sleep. I kept hearing noises."

Zoe and I looked at each other nervously.

Mom shrugged. "With the two of you outside, my imagination was working overtime. I kept picturing bears and cougars wandering into the yard. What they would be doing in the city, I have no idea. But there you go. I guess mothers are born to worry."

"Well, you didn't need to," I told her. "We never saw a single cougar or bear the whole night."

"There were a couple of squirrels running around in the tree for a while," Zoe added. "Maybe that's what you heard."

Across the table, I shot Zoe a *Are you crazy?* look. Then I said, "Yeah, Mom. The squirrels were pretty noisy. Not dangerous though. So can we sleep outside again?"

Mom sighed. "Oh, I suppose so."

Suddenly I had a thought. It seemed pretty unlikely, but maybe there was still a chance Mr. Dotty was innocent. "Hey, Dad," I said, "did the police catch the guy who robbed that bank in Winnipeg?"

His fork stopped halfway to his mouth, and he frowned. "To tell you the truth, Zach, I really don't know. I missed the news last night." Then he glanced at his watch. "But there should be a broadcast coming on right about now. C'mon. Let's check it out." Then he shoved the forkful of waffle into his mouth and pushed himself away from the table.

I dropped my napkin onto my plate and followed him into the living room.

Zoe started to leave the table too. "Not so fast, young lady," Mom said. "Finish your breakfast. If anything earth-shattering is going on in the world, I'm sure your father and brother will let you know."

The television came on to a commercial. After that it went right to the news. I listened hard. The reporter was talking about wars and floods and fires, and a bunch of political stuff I didn't understand. There was a story about a new drug that was supposed to cure cancer and another one about some company that had gone out of business, but nothing about the bank robbery in Winnipeg. After a while I started to think there wasn't going to be any news about it.

"... Contract talks between nurses and hospital management have come to a halt," the reporter said. "If a deal isn't reached by midnight, nurses could go on strike.

"On the environmental front, a local wetland is in danger of being destroyed. This could leave many species of animals homeless, including a wide variety of fish, insects, amphibians, mammals, and over 300 species of birds, such as herons and ducks."

"That's our marsh!" I shouted as a video jolted me to attention. "Zoe, come in here. Quick! The marsh is drying up!"

Zoe ran into the living room. "What?"

"Look!" I said, pointing to the television.

The video had switched to the Silver Ponds construction site. It had only been a little over a week since we'd been there, but it looked totally different. There were partly built houses all over the place.

The reporter was talking again. "This situation is the result of a recent housing development that has interfered with the wetland's natural water supply. Consequently, the area is drying up. If the weather stays warm, authorities predict there will be no water in the wetland by summer's end."

The video switched back to the marsh. It

looked terrible! The grass and bulrushes were turning brown and dry. And the pond had shrunk to half its size. In some places it was just mud, and there wasn't a single duck or heron anywhere.

"No water means no plant life," the reporter was saying, "and definitely no animals. Unless funding can be found to repair the damage done by bulldozers, residents can say goodbye to another natural habitat."

"No!" Zoe stomped her foot. "That can't happen. They can't let the marsh die!"

"It's pretty sad, all right," Dad sighed. "But you can't fight progress, honey. What's done is done."

Zoe stamped her foot again. "Killing the marsh isn't progress! Somebody should make those builder guys tear down the houses!"

"I don't think that would fix the problem," Dad explained patiently. "The marsh has to be reunited with its water supply, and that costs money."

Zoe dropped down onto the carpet beside me and glared at the news reporter as if it was his fault the marsh was drying up. I knew exactly how she felt. I was upset too.

I stared at the television until the news ended. There were lots of reports, but nothing about the bank robbery in Winnipeg. The weird thing is, it just didn't seem that important anymore. All I could think about was the marsh.

"C'mon," Zoe said, nudging me with her elbow. "Let's go outside."

The two of us shuffled off to the backyard like a couple of zombies and flopped down onto the back steps.

For a while we just sat there. We didn't say a word. What was there to say? We both felt horrible about the marsh, and talking about it would only make it worse. The marsh was drying up. Soon it would be nothing but dust and dead grass. Frogs and ducks and herons couldn't live without water. They'd have to leave. But where would they go?

"Do you think Mr. Dotty knows?" Zoe asked.

I shrugged. "I don't know. What do you think?"

Zoe shook her head. "I don't know either."

"I don't think he can know," I said finally. "If he did, he'd be marching around at the building site with a big sign, yelling at the construction people and getting in their way so they can't work."

"How do you know he *isn't* doing that?" Zoe shot back.

I nodded toward the fence. "Because he's in his yard. Listen. Can't you hear his wheelbarrow?"

Zoe tiptoed across the yard and spied between the fence boards. After a while I went over and joined her.

"Do you think we should go over there and tell him?" I asked.

Zoe shook her head. "We'd be wasting our time. Mr. Dotty would probably just yell at us again and tell us to go home. Ever since he robbed that bank, he's been different."

11

Trap Door Thieves

"Why are all these pillows here?" Zoe asked when she crawled into the tent that night. "I can barely get inside."

"They're camouflage," I told her, "in case Mom has trouble sleeping again and decides to check on us. We'll stuff our sleeping bags to make it look like we're in them, when really we'll be in Mr. Dotty's garage."

"You are getting to be a very sneaky person, Zach Gallagher." Zoe grinned.

I grinned back.

I guess I shouldn't have taken what Zoe said as a compliment. I mean, sneakiness isn't the sort of thing a person should be proud of. But seeing as

Zoe and I were trying to keep Mr. Dotty from going to jail, I figured a little sneakiness was okay.

By tomorrow the stolen money would be in a big red mailbox and things could start getting back to normal. Mr. Dotty could take the locks off his garage, and Zoe and I could go back to visiting him. No more secrets. No more sneaking around.

But first we had to get the money. I felt sort of guilty about that. It was kind of like now *we* were the ones who were crooks.

"Not really," Zoe argued, "because the money doesn't belong to Mr. Dotty. It belongs to the bank. We're not stealing it; we're giving it back. If you think about it, we're actually doing a good deed — *for everybody!* The bank gets its money, and Mr. Dotty stays out of jail."

* * *

Mom and Dad weren't in a hurry to go to bed, so it was almost midnight before Zoe and I could leave the tent. But since we'd made the same trip the night before, things moved a lot faster. Until a light went on in our house, that is.

I was just getting ready to drop the rope ladder through the trap door when the whole kitchen lit up.

"Someone's coming!" I hissed. "Quick. Turn off the flashlight and lie down!"

Zoe did. And not a second too soon either, because the next thing I knew, the back door opened and there was Mom. She'd just checked on us half an hour ago! Why was she doing it again?

I didn't move a muscle. I don't think I even breathed. I just pressed myself as flat as I could against the mossy roof and waited for her to look inside the tent. I had no idea what would happen if she discovered Zoe and I weren't in it, but I was pretty sure it wouldn't be good.

Mom crossed the grass, lifted the flap, and looked inside. I squeezed my eyes shut and said my prayers harder than I'd ever said them before. Right after I mouthed the word, *Amen*, she dropped the flap and walked back to the house.

But when she didn't go back inside, I started praying all over again. For the longest time nothing happened. Mom just stood on the back step, rubbing her arms and staring into the night. Maybe she was listening for bears and cougars — or squirrels. But it felt more like she was looking for Zoe and me. Mom always seems to know where we are and what we're doing. It's as if she has radar or X-ray vision or something. So when her gaze stopped right on Mr. Dotty's garage, I was sure she'd spotted us.

Zoe must've thought so too, because she gasped. Mom put her hand over her eyes and squinted harder in our direction. Had she heard Zoe? Had she seen us?

"Don't move." I barely breathed the words to Zoe.

Then Dad was at the door too! He put a hand on Mom's shoulder. "Come back to bed, Jan," he told her. "The kids are fine."

Mom looked up at him and sighed. "I guess you're right." Then she and Dad went back into the house. A few seconds later, the lights went out.

Zoe's whole body melted into the mossy roof. "Whew! That was close. What if Mom and Dad had checked our sleeping bags?"

"Don't even think about it," I shuddered.

Quieter than ever, we lowered the rope ladder and climbed down into the garage. We made sure to point the flashlight at the floor until we got to the bottom — just in case Mom was still prowling around the house and spying out windows.

The suitcase was right where it had been the night before. I'd thought Mr. Dotty might have moved it, so it was a big relief to see it sitting there. I knelt down to unlock it. The latches snapped open, and I pushed up the lid. Even though I knew what was inside, the sight of all that money made my heart pound all over again.

"What are you waiting for?" Zoe asked as she grabbed a stack of bills and shoved them into her backpack. "Mom might come back out. We have to hurry."

She was right. I slipped off my backpack and began filling it. As the stacks of money in the suitcase disappeared our backpacks got fatter and fatter. And heavier and heavier. Climbing out of Mr. Dotty's garage and down the tree was going to be harder than I'd thought.

"Money sure weighs a lot," Zoe muttered as she struggled to lift her pack off the floor.

Before I could answer, a beam of light flashed behind us, and a voice said, "Indeed it does, Zoe. Indeed it does."

12

Caught!

I spun toward the light. It was like looking into a giant sparkler. Yellow spears stabbed my eyes through the blackness. There was no way to see past them to the person holding the flashlight. Not that it mattered. I knew who it was.

"Mr. Dotty?" Zoe said cautiously. "Is that you?"

The flashlight beam moved from our eyes to the floor. It was Mr. Dotty all right, and he did not look happy to see us.

Zoe didn't seem to notice. "What are you doing out here?" she demanded.

The stern look on Mr. Dotty's face got even sterner. "This is my property," he said. His voice wasn't the least bit friendly. In fact, it was downright *un*friendly. It was the sort of voice that could belong to a bank robber, and for the first time, I felt a little afraid of Mr. Dotty.

He took a step toward us. We took a step back.

"The real question is what are *you* doing out here?" he growled. "It is the middle of the night, and you are breaking the law. What would your parents say if they knew you'd broken into my garage? I have half a mind to take you to them right this minute." His eyes, which had narrowed, looked at the empty suitcase and then our bulging backpacks. Talk about being caught red-handed!

"It's not what you're thinking," I stammered.

Mr. Dotty's eyes became even squintier. "And exactly what am I thinking, young Zach? Hmm?"

I opened my mouth to answer, but Zoe beat me to it. "You've been hiding in here, waiting for us!" she huffed, jamming her fists onto her hips and frowning. "You ambushed us! That is so sneaky!"

Mr. Dotty blinked in disbelief. Zoe made it sound like he was the one who'd done something wrong. Actually, considering he'd robbed a bank, he *had* done something wrong. But at the moment it was Zoe and I who'd been caught, so from Mr. Dotty's point of view, *we* were thieves too.

"How did you even know we were going to be here?" I said.

He glanced up at the trap door. "You left a calling card."

"A calling card?" Zoe repeated curiously.

Mr. Dotty nodded. "This morning when I came to clean up the glass from a dish I presumed Mila had broken — "

"Mila *did* break it," Zoe said.

Mr. Dotty cleared his throat. "As I was saying, when I cleaned up the broken glass, I discovered several tufts of moss on the floor directly under the trap door. There is only one place the moss could have come from, and that's the roof. Clearly, someone had broken into the garage. I confess I wasn't sure you were the culprits, but since you were camping in your backyard last night, you were definitely suspects."

"But that was last night. How did you know we'd come back?" I asked.

Mr. Dotty shrugged. "I didn't. Not for certain.

But I saw you were sleeping outdoors again tonight, so I believed there was a good chance. I thought your break-and-enter adventure was just curiosity. You wanted to know why I'd locked my garage." His eyes moved to our money-stuffed backpacks again. "And now you know."

In the movies, that's when Mr. Dotty would have pulled a gun and waved it at us, saying we knew too much for our own good. But he didn't. He just shook his head, sighed, and slumped against the chest of drawers.

"Now that you children know my secret, the whole world is going to find out, and my life is never going to be the same. I wish I had never set eyes on that money. If I could give it back, I would."

I couldn't believe my ears! A huge wave of relief washed over me. In my heart I'd known all along Mr. Dotty wasn't a thief. He'd just had a weak moment. But he was over it now. He wanted to give the money back. And Zoe and I could help him.

Zoe started hopping around and clapping her

hands. "Oh, Mr. Dotty, that's wonderful!"

Mr. Dotty frowned. "What's so wonderful about it?"

"Because Zach and I can help you. We have a plan. Don't you see? That's why we broke into your garage. That's why we were putting the money into our backpacks. We were going to give it back."

I nodded enthusiastically. "That's right. We were going to give the money back to the bank, so you wouldn't have to go to jail."

Mr. Dotty now looked more confused than ever. "Bank? Jail? What are you children talking about?"

Zoe walked over to Mr. Dotty and put a reassuring hand on his arm. "It's okay, Mr. Dotty. You don't have to keep it a secret anymore. You don't have to worry about going to jail either. Zach and I would never tell the police on you, no matter how many banks you robbed."

Mr. Dotty's mouth actually dropped open.

"It's okay," Zoe assured him again, giving his arm another pat.

Finally Mr. Dotty closed his mouth. He looked from Zoe to me and back again. "You think I robbed a bank?"

Zoe glanced at me and rolled her eyes. "He's in denial," she whispered.

"We saw it on the news, Mr. Dotty," I said. "It was on videotape and everything. You robbed that bank in Winnipeg. We saw you." I glanced toward our backpacks. "There's the proof."

Mr. Dotty's mouth dropped open again. Then it closed. Then it opened. It went on like that for almost a minute — Mr. Dotty opening and shutting his mouth like a fish gulping for air. Finally his face broke into the biggest grin I've ever seen, and he started to laugh. Once he got going, he couldn't seem to stop. He just staggered all over the garage, holding his sides and shaking with laughter.

"Ssshhh," I said. I was afraid he was going to wake up Mom and Dad.

"I don't see what's so funny," Zoe grumbled.

Laughed out at last, Mr. Dotty crumpled to the garage floor. "Oh, children," he panted, "I'm sorry. You must think I'm a lunatic." He grinned and gulped some more as he tried to catch his breath. "But I'm not. Not really. And you'll be happy to know I didn't rob that bank either."

"You didn't?" I really wanted to believe Mr. Dotty, but how could I? I pointed to our backpacks. "But what about all this money?"

Mr. Dotty put a finger to his lips. "It's a secret," he said. "If I tell you, you can't say a word to anyone. Promise?"

Zoe and I nodded.

"All right then." He leaned in close and whispered in our ears, "I won the lottery."

13

The Truth

"The lottery!" Zoe and I yelled at the same time.

Mr. Dotty nodded.

Zoe's eyes got round as golf balls. "You won $250,000?"

Mr. Dotty's eyebrows bunched up. "Yes. Well, almost — but how did you know?"

Zoe looked down at her feet, "That's how much was stolen in the bank robbery." Obviously she still wasn't sure Mr. Dotty was telling the truth. I hate to admit it, but I wasn't either.

Mr. Dotty closed his eyes and shook his head. "How many times do I have to tell you, I did not rob that bank! The police captured the real thief this afternoon — money and all. It was all people talked about at the bank today."

Zoe perked up. "Really?"

"Really," Mr. Dotty harrumphed. He gestured toward our backpacks. "*This* is lottery money. $237,440.86." He paused and frowned. "Well, not exactly that much. Not anymore, anyway. Now it's just $237,400. I spent $40.86. And if I don't find a way to get rid of the rest of it, I'll probably end up spending even more!"

Zoe and I looked at each other, puzzled.

"What's wrong with that?" I asked. "It's your money. You're allowed to spend it. Why would you want to get rid of it?"

"And why did you buy a lottery ticket in the first place if you didn't want to win?" Zoe chimed in.

Mr. Dotty jumped up and started pacing. "I *didn't* buy a ticket! My sister bought it. Don't you remember? It was in the birthday card she sent, along with the photograph of her dog."

I nodded. "Oh, yeah. I remember. That was a pretty funny-looking dog."

Mr. Dotty cleared his throat. "Yes, well, the

point is I won. And since my sister purchased the ticket in Winnipeg when she was on holiday, that's where I had to go to cash it in. I didn't win the big prize — thank goodness — but I won enough to make life difficult."

Zoe stepped in front of him, forcing him to stop walking. "What are you talking about, Mr. Dotty? The money will make life easier for you — not harder. Now you won't have to shop at thrift stores. You won't have to take bottles and pop cans to the recycling depot either. Heck, you could even buy a car."

Mr. Dotty started pacing again. "It just so happens I *like* shopping at thrift stores," he fumed. "Not only do I pay less, but I get what I need *and* I'm recycling. Most of the items at thrift stores are in perfectly good condition. The only reason people throw them away is because they want something new. As for bottles and cans, collecting them keeps the environment clean, and taking them to a recycling depot means they'll be reused instead of being heaped in a landfill." He scowled at Zoe. "As for buying a car, how many times have I told you how harmful motor vehicles are? It's bad enough their exhaust fumes destroy the ozone. I don't even want to think about how they're using up the earth's fossil fuels. At the rate people are going, the world soon won't be fit for a living thing. Every man, woman, and child needs to be more conscious of the earth's resources and — "

I knew I shouldn't interrupt, but I also knew that once Mr. Dotty got wound up about the environment, he could go on for hours. And we didn't have that kind of time. "So what *would* you like to buy with the money?" I said.

"Nothing." He crossed his arms over his chest and shook his head stubbornly. "Absolutely nothing."

"There must be something you want or need," I tried again. "A new shovel or hose maybe? Seeds for your garden?"

"New pajamas to wear when you do tychee?" That was Zoe.

"Cat toys for Mila?"

Mr. Dotty clucked his tongue and shook his

head. "No, no, no. I can buy those things with the money I earn at the bank."

"Well, how about a new roof for your garage then?" Zoe suggested. "The one you have now is all covered with moss. And it's really slippery. Do you know how dangerous that is, Mr. Dotty? Zach and I could have fallen off and hurt ourselves! Died even!"

Mr. Dotty raised an eyebrow at Zoe. "A very good reason not to be on my roof then, I would say."

"Okay, so you don't need the money," I said. "Then why not just put it in the bank in case you do need it one day?"

Mr. Dotty sighed. "If I did that, everyone would know about it."

"So what?"

"I've worked at the bank a very long time. I've seen what happens when ordinary people come into a lot of money. They become consumed with buying things — things they neither need nor want. But they can't seem to help themselves.

"To make matters worse, all their friends and

family — even perfect strangers — start asking them for money. If the person doesn't share, he's hated; if he does share, people just keep asking for more until there is no money left. Either way, it's a life of misery." He shook his head. "No thank you. I don't wish to live like that."

"You could give the money to your sister," Zoe said.

"Now why would I want to do that?" he demanded. "I love my sister. I don't want her to be miserable either."

"So you're just going to keep the money in your garage?"

Mr. Dotty shrugged. "I suppose so — for the time being anyway. At least until I can think of something else to do with it."

"You could burn it," Zoe suggested. "That would get rid of it."

Mr. Dotty gasped. "Then I *would* go to jail. Destroying money is a federal offence. Never mind. My brain is a bit bogged down at the moment, but I'll think of something. You don't need to — "

"The marsh!" I remembered, and leaped into the air. "That's it! You can give it to the marsh."

14

Problem Solved

Zoe and Mr. Dotty both turned and blinked at me.

"What are you talking about?" Mr. Dotty asked.

"Yeah, Zach," Zoe frowned. "What are you talking about?"

"Don't you get it?" I couldn't stop grinning. "The marsh. The marsh! Mr. Dotty can fix the marsh!"

"How?" asked Zoe.

I rolled my eyes. "Don't you remember the news reporter saying the marsh was going to dry up *unless* it could be reconnected with its water supply?"

Zoe was still frowning, but she nodded. "Yeah. So?"

"*So* that's going to cost money — *lots* of money."

Zoe's face cleared and she started bouncing up and down. "Mr. Dotty's money!" she exclaimed.

"Exactly."

Mr. Dotty cleared his throat. "I hate to interrupt this little celebration," he said, "but would one of you kindly tell me what you're talking about?"

Zoe turned to look at him. "We're talking about the marsh," she said. "It's dying. Didn't you know?"

"I beg your pardon? What do you mean *the marsh is dying?*"

"We saw it on the news this morning," I said. My brain was going a million miles a minute, and I couldn't get the words out fast enough. "We were watching to find out about the bank robbery, and the news guy started talking about the marsh. He said the new Silver Ponds housing development had cut off the marsh's water supply, and because of that, the marsh is drying up."

"What?" Mr. Dotty could barely talk.

"It's true," Zoe said. "There was video and everything. The marsh looks terrible! The water in the pond is really low, and all the plants are dying. The reporter said the animals were going to have to find some other place to live."

Mr. Dotty sank onto a stack of old phonograph records.

"I can't believe it," he croaked. "That marsh is a landmark. Those birds and animals, the fish, the insects," he spread his arms in disbelief. "They've lived there forever. Where will they go? What will happen to them? This is terrible!"

I grabbed Mr. Dotty's arm and dragged him back to his feet. "Maybe not," I told him. "The news reporter also said the marsh could be saved if it could get reconnected to its water supply. But doing that was going to cost a lot of money — money the government doesn't have … but you do."

By the time Zoe and I got back to our tent, it was nearly two in the morning. We should have been exhausted, but we were too excited to sleep. Mr. Dotty wasn't a thief after all. He was a lottery winner. And he was going to use his winnings to save the marsh. Everything bad was turning out good.

*   *   *

The Wildlife Preservation Society — they're the people who were going to fix the marsh — came and picked up Mr. Dotty's suitcase of money the very next day. And was Mr. Dotty ever happy! For most people, winning the lottery is a dream, but for Mr. Dotty it had been more like a nightmare. All I know is that after he gave the money away he smiled nonstop for days. And the really great thing was that his money was saving the marsh he loved.

Zoe and I wanted to go and see it. But Mr. Dotty said it would be too upsetting; it would be better to wait until it was fixed. But even after the marsh had water in it again, Mr. Dotty still made us wait. And that was really hard, because I'm not very good at waiting. Zoe is even worse.

Then suddenly, one day it was time. Zoe and I

had just started up Mr. Dotty's driveway when we spotted him standing in his garage with his binoculars around his neck and his checklist in his hand. That could mean only one thing.

"Finally!" he complained as we ran up to meet him. "I thought I was going to have to go to the marsh without you."

"No way." I grinned. Zoe just squealed and started bouncing around like a baby kangaroo.

Mr. Dotty didn't waste a minute getting down to business. "Cameras," he called, and Zoe and I instantly raced for the shelf where they were kept.

"I get the — " Zoe began, but then stopped. Her feet stopped too, which is why I ran into the back of her. But she didn't even notice. "Where did all the cameras go?" she squeaked.

I looked at the shelf, and that's when I realized what had made Zoe put on the brakes. All Mr. Dotty's old cameras were gone — every single one. There *were* two new cameras on the shelf, but I'd never seen them before.

I looked from Mr. Dotty to the cameras and

then back again. "I don't get it." I shook my head and frowned.

"Me neither," Zoe said.

Mr. Dotty chuckled and walked over to us. "It's really very simple," he explained as he picked up the cameras and handed one to each of us. "These are the cameras you're going to use today when we go to the marsh. A gift from me to you."

I could feel my eyes starting to bug out. "We get to keep them?"

"But they're brand new," Zoe said. "And they even have film in them."

"You're absolutely correct," he replied. "Today I thought it would be a good idea to take some real photographs. We came so close to losing the marsh, I wanted us to have a permanent reminder — in pictures — of how precious it is. And, yes, the cameras are yours to keep." Then he tousled my hair. "So, come on. Are we going to the marsh or not?"

As I slipped the camera around my neck and watched Mr. Dotty march down the driveway, I wondered how I could ever have thought he was

111

a crook.

"Hey, Mr. Dotty," I called. As he turned around, I raised my camera. "Smile!"